亲爱的爸爸妈妈们：

在阅读这本书之前，您可以让您的孩子先在左侧的横线上写下自己的名字——这可能成为他（她）完完整整读完的第一本书，也因此成为真正意义上第一本属于他（她）自己的书。

作为美国最知名的儿童启蒙阅读丛书"I Can Read!"中的一册，它专为刚开始阅读起步的孩子量身打造，具有用词简单、句子简短、适当重复，以及注重语言的韵律和节奏等特点。这些特点非常有助于孩子对语言的学习，不论是学习母语，还是学习作为第二语言的英语。

故事的主角是鼎鼎大名的贝贝熊一家，这一风靡美国近半个世纪的形象对孩子具有天然的亲和力，很多跟贝贝熊有关的故事都为孩子所津津乐道。作为双语读物，它不但能引导孩子独立捧起书本，去了解书中有趣的情节，还能做到真正从兴趣出发，让孩子领略到英语学习的乐趣。

就从贝贝熊开始，让您的孩子爱上阅读，帮助他们开启自己的双语阅读之旅吧！

图书在版编目（CIP）数据

小马驹奥斯卡：英汉对照 / (美) 博丹(Berenstain,J.)，(美) 博丹 (Berenstain,M.) 著；
姚雁青译. — 乌鲁木齐：新疆青少年出版社，2013.1
（贝贝熊系列丛书）

ISBN 978-7-5515-2742-2

Ⅰ.①小… Ⅱ.①博… ②博… ③姚… Ⅲ.①英语－汉语－对照读物②儿童故事－
美国－现代 Ⅳ.①H319.4：I

中国版本图书馆CIP数据核字(2012)第273214号

版权登记：图字 29-2012-24

The Berenstain Bears and the Shaggy Little Pony
copyright©2011 by Berenstain Bears, Inc.
This edition arranged with Sterling Lord Literistic, Inc.
through Andrew Nurnberg Associates International Limited

贝贝熊系列丛书
小马驹奥斯卡

(美) 简·博丹 麦克·博丹 绘著 Jan & Mike Berenstain 姚雁青 译

出 版 人 徐 江　　　　　　　　　　策 　 划 许国萍
责任编辑 贺艳华　　　　　　　　　　美术编辑 查 璇 刘小珍
法律顾问 钟 麟 13201203567（新疆国法律师事务所）

新疆青少年出版社
（地址：乌鲁木齐市北京北路29号 邮编：830012）
Http://www.qingshao.net　　E-mail：QSbeijing@hotmail.com

印　　刷 北京时尚印佳彩色印刷有限公司　　经 　 销 全国新华书店
开　　本 787mm×1092mm　1/16　　　　印 　 张 2
版　　次 2013年1月第1版　　　　　　　　印 　 次 2013年1月第1次印刷
印　　数 1-10000册　　　　　　　　　　定 　 价 9.00元
标准书号 ISBN 978-7-5515-2742-2

制售盗版必究 举报查实奖励:0991-7833932 版权保护办公室举报电话：0991-7833927
销售热线:010-84853493 84851485 如有印刷装订质量问题 印刷厂负责掉换

The Berenstain Bears

I Can Read!

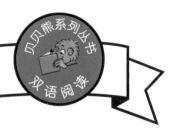

貝贝熊系列丛书 双语阅读

and the
Shaggy Little Pony
小马驹奥斯卡

(美) 简·博丹 麦克·博丹 绘著
Jan & Mike Berenstain

姚雁青 译

CHISO 新疆青少年出版社
SINCE 1956

Sister and Brother were visiting
their neighbor Farmer Ben.
They liked to help him take care of
the animals on his farm.

小熊妹妹和小熊哥哥在邻居农场主本先生那儿做客。
他们很喜欢帮本先生照料农场里的动物。

"Hello, cubs!" said Farmer Ben.
"I want you to meet someone new
on the farm."
He led them to a pen.
Inside was a shaggy little pony.

"小熊们，你们好！"农场主本先生招呼道，
"我想让你们见见农场里来的新伙计。"
他把他们领到一个围栏边，
那里面有一匹小马驹，全身的毛乱蓬蓬的。

"Meet old Oscar," said Ben.
"He has just come to live here."

"来认识一下老奥斯卡吧，"本先生说，
"他刚来这儿不久。"

"He is so cute!" said Sister.

The cubs rubbed his nose.

Oscar blew gently on their hands.

"That means he likes you," Ben told them.

"Can we help take care of him?"

asked Brother.

"Of course," said Ben.

"I will show you how."

"他好可爱啊！"小熊妹妹嚷道。
小熊们抚摸着他的鼻子，
奥斯卡轻柔地往他们的手上吹气。
本先生告诉小熊们："这说明他喜欢你们。"
小熊哥哥问："我们可以帮忙照顾他吗？"
"当然行啦！"本先生回答，"我来教你们怎么做。"

8

Brother and Sister gave water to Oscar.

They gave hay and feed to Oscar.

They washed Oscar.

They brushed Oscar.

小熊哥哥和小熊妹妹给奥斯卡提水喝。

他们拿来干草喂奥斯卡。

他们给奥斯卡洗澡。

他们给奥斯卡刷毛。

They led him into the barn.
They cleaned out his stall.
They picked out his hooves.

他们把他牵进马棚。
他们把他的棚栏打扫干净。
他们替他挑选马掌。

"That was a lot of work," said Ben.
"You did a good job.
Would you like to ride Oscar now?"
"Ride him?" said Sister.
"Could we?" said Brother.
"Why not?" said Ben.

"这活儿可不少啊，你们干得真不赖。"本先生表扬小熊们，
"现在，你们想骑奥斯卡遛遛吗？"
"骑他？"小熊妹妹惊喜地问。
"我们可以骑吗？"小熊哥哥问。
"为什么不呢？"本先生乐了。

Ben put an old saddle and bridle on Oscar.
He had riding helmets for the cubs to wear.

本先生给奥斯卡戴上一套旧的笼头和马鞍。
他拿出骑士头盔让小熊们戴上。

First, Ben helped Sister up onto Oscar.
He led Oscar and Sister around the pen.
Oscar was very calm and quiet.

首先，本先生帮小熊妹妹骑到了奥斯卡背上。
他带着奥斯卡和小熊妹妹绕着围栏转起了圈。
奥斯卡表现得又乖又安静。

Then it was Brother's turn.

"That was fun!" said Brother.

"Can we do it again tomorrow?" asked Sister.

"Why not?" said Farmer Ben.

接着，再换小熊哥哥骑。

"太好玩了！"小熊哥哥兴奋地叫着。

"我们明天能再来骑他吗？"小熊妹妹问。

"为什么不呢？"农场主本先生回答。

Brother and Sister began to go
to the farm every day.
They took care of Oscar
and they rode Oscar.
Soon they could ride him
without any help.
They rode him all over the farm.

小熊哥哥和小熊妹妹从此每天都到农场来。
他们细心地照料奥斯卡，还练习骑马。
很快，他们不需要任何帮助就可以自己骑了。
他们骑着奥斯卡在农场里到处转悠。

They loved Oscar
and they loved to ride him.

他们喜欢极了奥斯卡，
他们也喜欢骑着他到处跑。

One day, the cubs saw a sign
on the side of Farmer Ben's barn:

一天，小熊们看到农场主本先生的谷仓侧面贴了一张告示，
上面写着：明天有马术表演，欢迎小熊们踊跃参加，备有大奖若干。

"What does that mean?"
they asked Farmer Ben.
"There's going to be a riding show
for cubs, here," said Ben.
"The best riders will get prize ribbons."
"Can we be in the show?" they asked.
"Why not?" said Ben.

"那是什么意思？"他们问农场主本先生。
"这儿将要为小熊们举办一场马术表演，"本先生回答，
"那些最好的骑手们将得到奖章。"
"我们可以参加吗？"小熊们跃跃欲试。
"为什么不呢？"本先生鼓励他们。

The next day, there were lots of riders
and ponies at the farm.
Some of the ponies were very fancy.
Some of the riders wore fancy clothes.

第二天，农场里来了许多骑手，还有他们的小马。
有些小马看上去特别神气活现。
有些骑手打扮得也很神气活现。

Brother and Sister were worried.
How would they do
on their shaggy little pony?
"Don't worry," said Ben.
"Oscar will do fine."

小熊哥哥和小熊妹妹不由得担心起来，
他们该拿自己乱蓬蓬的小马驹怎么办？
本先生安慰他们："别担心，奥斯卡会好好表现的。"

The fancy ponies and the fancy riders
went first.

那些神气活现的小马和神气活现的骑手先出场了。

They rode around in front of the judges.
The judges watched how they rode.

他们在裁判面前兜起了圈。
裁判们观察着他们的骑术。

23

But it was a windy day.

Leaves swirled around the ponies' legs.

The fancy ponies were scared.

They bucked and kicked.

The judges frowned and made notes on their pads.

但是这天有风。

树叶绕着小马们的腿打起转来。

那些神气活现的小马害怕了。

它们又是乱蹦，又是尥蹶子。

裁判们皱起眉头，在他们的记分牌上做了记录。

Then it was time
for Brother and Sister to ride.
They took turns on Oscar.
The wind and the leaves
did not bother Oscar.

轮到小熊哥哥和小熊妹妹出场了。
他们轮流骑着奥斯卡上场表演。
奥斯卡一点儿也不在乎呼啸的风和乱舞的树叶。

He was quiet and calm.

He trotted in front of the judges.

The judges smiled and nodded.

他表现得安静又从容。

他在裁判面前优雅地一溜小跑。

裁判们微笑着点头称赞。

All the ponies and riders lined up.

The judges brought out the prize ribbons.

Blue was for first place.

Red was for second place.

Yellow was for third place.

所有的小马和骑手排成一列，
裁判们拿出奖章准备颁奖。
蓝色的奖章是给第一名的。
红色的奖章是给第二名的。
黄色的奖章是给第三名的。

White was for fourth place.

Brother and Sister had their fingers crossed.

"I hope we get a ribbon," Sister said.

白色的奖章是给第四名的。

小熊哥哥和小熊妹妹交叉起手指，祈求好运。

"我希望我们能得到一个奖章。"小熊妹妹说。

The judges pinned the blue ribbon
on Oscar's bridle.
Sister and Brother were tied
for first place!
"I told you nothing bothers old Oscar,"
said Farmer Ben.

裁判把蓝色的奖章拴在了奥斯卡的笼头上。
小熊哥哥和小熊妹妹得了并列第一！
农场主本先生骄傲地说："我告诉过你们，
什么都难不住我们的老奥斯卡！"

Brother and Sister rubbed Oscar's nose.
Oscar blew gently on their hands.

小熊哥哥和小熊妹妹抚摸着奥斯卡的鼻子。
奥斯卡轻柔地往他们的手上吹气。

亲爱的爸爸妈妈们：

  在阅读这本书之前，您可以让您的孩子先在左侧的横线上写下自己的名字——这可能成为他（她）完完整整读完的第一本书，也因此成为真正意义上第一本属于他（她）自己的书。

  作为美国最知名的儿童启蒙阅读丛书"I Can Read!"中的一册，它专为刚开始阅读起步的孩子量身打造，具有用词简单、句子简短、适当重复，以及注重语言的韵律和节奏等特点。这些特点非常有助于孩子对语言的学习，不论是学习母语，还是学习作为第二语言的英语。

  故事的主角是鼎鼎大名的贝贝熊一家，这一风靡美国近半个世纪的形象对孩子具有天然的亲和力，很多跟贝贝熊有关的故事都为孩子所津津乐道。作为双语读物，它不但能引导孩子独立捧起书本，去了解书中有趣的情节，还能做到真正从兴趣出发，让孩子领略到英语学习的乐趣。

  就从贝贝熊开始，让您的孩子爱上阅读，帮助他们开启自己的双语阅读之旅吧！

图书在版编目（CIP）数据

参观养蜂场：汉英对照 / （美）博丹（Berenstain,J.），（美）博丹（Berenstain,M.）
著；姚雁青译. —乌鲁木齐：新疆青少年出版社，2013.1
　　（贝贝熊系列丛书）

ISBN 978-7-5515-2741-5

Ⅰ.①参… Ⅱ.①博… ②博… ③姚… Ⅲ.①英语－汉语－对照读物②儿童故
事－美国－现代 Ⅳ.①H319.4：I

中国版本图书馆CIP数据核字(2012)第273210号

版权登记：图字 29-2012-24

The Berenstain Bears' Class Trip
copyright©2009 by Berenstain Bears, Inc.
This edition arranged with Sterling Lord Literistic, Inc.
through Andrew Nurnberg Associates International Limited

贝贝熊系列丛书
参观养蜂场

（美）简·博丹　麦克·博丹　绘著　Jan & Mike Berenstain　　姚雁青　译

出 版 人　徐　江　　　　　　　　　　策　　划　许国萍
责任编辑　贺艳华　　　　　　　　　　美术编辑　查　璇　　刘小珍
法律顾问　钟　麟 13201203567（新疆国法律师事务所）

新疆青少年出版社
（地址：乌鲁木齐市北京北路29号　邮编：830012）

Http://www.qingshao.net　　E-mail：QSbeijing@hotmail.com

印　　刷　北京时尚印佳彩色印刷有限公司　　经　　销　全国新华书店
开　　本　787mm×1092mm　1/16　　　　　印　　张　2
版　　次　2013年1月第1版　　　　　　　　印　　次　2013年1月第1次印刷
印　　数　1-10000册　　　　　　　　　　　定　　价　9.00元
标准书号　ISBN 978-7-5515-2741-5

制售盗版必究 举报查实奖励:0991-7833932　　版权保护办公室举报电话:0991-7833927
销售热线:010-84853493 84851485　　　如有印刷装订质量问题 印刷厂负责掉换

The Berenstain Bears'

I Can Read!

贝贝熊系列丛书 双语阅读

Class Trip
参观养蜂场

(美) 简·博丹　麦克·博丹　绘著
Jan & Mike Berenstain

姚雁青　译

CHISO 新疆青少年出版社

Brother Bear's class is going on a trip.
The class is going to a honey farm.

小熊哥哥的班级组织活动。
他们要去参观养蜂场。

Mama and Papa Bear are
teacher's helpers on the trip.

熊妈妈和熊爸爸是这次活动的家长义工。

"Mmm," says Papa Bear, licking his lips.
"I hope they give out free samples."
"I am sure they do," says Mama Bear.
Sister Bear is going, too.
There is an extra seat on the bus
next to Teacher Bob.

熊爸爸舔了舔嘴唇说:"嗯,我希望他们能给些赠品尝尝。"
熊妈妈回答:"他们一定会给的。"
小熊妹妹也来了。
她坐在鲍勃老师旁边多出来的座位上。

Honey Bear will stay at home
with Gramps and Gran.

熊宝宝留在家里，和熊爷爷、熊奶奶在一起。

The bus is on its way.

"Let's all sing!" says Cousin Fred.

"Ninety-nine jars of honey on the wall . . ."

sings the class.

Papa Bear joins in.

校车向养蜂场开去。

弗雷德表哥提议："我们唱歌吧！"

"墙上挂了九十九罐蜂蜜……" 全班同学一起大声唱。

熊爸爸也跟着哼起来。

"Are we almost there?" asks Sister.

"Almost!" answers Papa.

They see a sign:

BEAR COUNTRY HONEY FARM, NEXT EXIT.

"Hooray!" yells the class.

小熊妹妹问："我们快到了吗？"
熊爸爸回答："快了！"
他们看见了路标：
　"下一个出口——熊王国养蜂场"。
大家欢呼起来："太棒了！"

Brother Bear sniffs the air.

"Smell that?" he says. "Honey!"

They all take a deep breath.

"Mmm!" They sigh.

小熊哥哥使劲吸了吸鼻子："你们闻到了吗？蜂蜜的味道！"
大家都深吸了口气，陶醉地说："嗯，真香！"

"I can almost taste that honey now,"
says Papa, licking his lips again.
"Look! We are here!" says Sister.

"我好像已经尝到了蜂蜜的味道。"熊爸爸又舔了舔嘴唇。
"看哪！我们到了！"小熊妹妹叫起来。

12

They all get off the bus.
Teacher Bob leads the way.
They see a huge field of beehives.
The sound of buzzing bees fills the air.

大家都下了车。
鲍勃老师在前面带路。
一路上大家看到了许许多多的蜂箱，
到处是蜜蜂飞舞的嗡嗡声。

13

"Over there is the clover field,"
says Teacher Bob.
"Thousands of bees gather nectar there.
They bring it back to the hives
and make it into honey."

鲍勃老师说："那边是三叶草地,
成千上万只蜜蜂在那里采集花蜜。
然后,它们把花蜜带回蜂箱,酿成蜂蜜。"

"How do they do that?" asks Brother.

小熊哥哥好奇地问：“它们是怎么酿蜜的呢？”

"Look," says Teacher Bob.

He points to a hive.

"You can see for yourself."

"瞧,"鲍勃老师指着一个蜂箱说,

"你可以自己去观察。"

One of the hives has a glass side.
The cubs can see the bees making honey.

有一只蜂箱其中一面是用玻璃做的，
透过玻璃，小熊们可以看到蜜蜂如何酿蜜。

"See that big bee?" says Papa.
"That is the queen."

"看见那只大蜜蜂了吗？" 熊爸爸说，"那是蜂后。"

"Correct," says Teacher Bob.
"All the others are her children."
"Wow," says Sister.
"She has more children
than the Old Bear in the Shoe!"

"没错！"鲍勃老师接着说，"其他所有的蜜蜂都是她的后代。"
"哇，她的孩子可真多！比《老熊住在鞋里面》老熊家的孩子
还要多啊！"小熊妹妹惊叹道。

"How do you get the honey
out of the hive?" asks Brother.
"I'll show you," says Papa.
He lifts the lid of a hive.

小熊哥哥又问："怎么才能把蜂蜜从蜂箱里取出来呢？"
"我演示给你们看。"熊爸爸说着，抬起一个蜂箱的盖子。

"No! No!" says Teacher Bob.
A huge cloud of bees flies out.

鲍勃老师赶紧制止他："别打开！别打开！"
话音未落，一大群黑压压的蜜蜂已经飞了出来。

"Follow me!" shouts Teacher Bob.

"跟我来!"鲍勃老师赶忙喊道。

All the bears run into the honey barn.
Teacher Bob slams the door shut
just in time.
"Now you will see the correct way
to get the honey out," he says.

等大家都逃进蜂蜜仓库，
鲍勃老师马上砰地关上门。
"现在，你们可以观察取出蜂蜜的正确方法了！"他说。

The cubs look out the window.
Beekeepers are gathering honey.
They wear special suits and hats
to keep from getting stung.

小熊们朝窗外望去。
养蜂熊正在收集蜂蜜。
他们穿着特制的衣服，戴着头罩，以防被蜜蜂蜇到。

First, the beekeepers blow smoke into
the hives to make the bees sleepy.
Then they lift out the honeycombs.

首先，养蜂熊往蜂箱里吹进一种烟雾，
把蜜蜂熏得晕乎乎的想睡觉。
然后，他们取出蜂巢。

They bring the honeycombs into the barn.

They put them on a big wheel.

They turn the crank.

他们把蜂巢拿到仓库里，

把它们放到一个大转盘上，

然后摇动手柄，使转盘转动起来。

Golden honey pours into a big vat.
Papa cannot wait to taste the honey.
He leans over too far and gets
honey all over himself.

金黄色的蜂蜜于是缓缓流进一个大桶。
熊爸爸迫不及待地想尝尝鲜。
他使劲地弯腰往桶里够，结果弄得浑身上下都是蜜。

"While Papa Bear is getting cleaned up,
you may all have some honey samples,"
says Teacher Bob.

"在给熊爸爸擦洗干净的时候,
你们都可以来点儿新鲜蜂蜜尝尝!"鲍勃老师宣布。

"Yea!" cry the cubs.

小熊们欢呼起来："耶，好棒啊！"

The class is back on the bus heading home.
Mama Bear says, "I saved a honey
sample for you, Papa dear."

参观结束，同学们坐上校车回家。
熊妈妈说："亲爱的熊爸，我给你留了一小瓶蜂蜜，你尝尝。"

"No, thank you," says Papa.
"I have already had my sample!"

"谢谢你，不用了，"熊爸爸不好意思地说，
"我已经尝过我那一份儿啦！"